JANE SEYMOUR · JAMES KEACH

THIS ONE 'N THAT ONE

in

Fried Pies
And Roast Cake

illustrated by Geoffrey Planer

ANGEL GATE
Los Angeles

Angel Gate, a division of Left Field Ink, Inc.
3111 W. Burbank Blvd., Suite 103, Burbank, CA 91505
Printed in China.
Designed by Claire Moore. Text set in Gill Sans.
Library of Congress Cataloging-in-publication Data
Seymour, Jane. /Fried Pies and Roast Cake
Jane Seymour and James Keach; illustrated by Geoffrey Planer.
p. cm. (This One and That One)
Summary: The kittens learn to negotiate as they decide
what to ask Mom to make for lunch.
[1. Cats-Fiction. 2. Brother -Fiction. 3. Food-Fiction.]
I. Keach, James. II. Planer, Geoffrey, ill. III. Title IV.
Series PZ7.S5235Tj 1998
Library of Congress Control Number: 2003093065
ISBN 1-932431-10-1

To
Kris and John
Kalen, Katie, Jenni, Sean, Thea, Erica,
Nina, Tom and Fizzy,
our inspirational friend Christopher Reeve, and
Jan of course!
And all the kids and kits around the world!

"Bless my purple paws - it's half past lunchtime!" said Lady Jane.

"My tummy's talking!" said **THIS ONE** .

"My tummy's shouting!" said **THAT ONE** .

"What would you like for lunch then?" asked Lady Jane.

"I'd like .....

     Cheese pies,

     And toffee cake,

     French fries,

     And chocolate shake,"

said **THIS ONE**.

"Well I'd like .....

     Roast potatoes,

     Lemon mousse,

     Chopped tomatoes,

     Orange juice,"

said **THAT ONE**.

"I don't have time to make two lunches guys," said Lady Jane. "Please help Mom and choose the same thing."

THIS ONE looked at **THAT ONE** and said:
"OK Mom. I've decided. We'll have ....

      Cheese pies,

      And toffee cake,

      French fries,

      And chocolate shake."

Then **THAT ONE** looked at **THIS ONE** and said,
"No, I've decided. We're going to have .....

      Roast potatoes,

      Lemon mousse,

      Chopped tomatoes,

      Orange juice."

"Listen kits, you better go and decide together now," said Lady Jane.

THIS ONE stood on a chair and shouted

"Cheese pies!
Toffee cake!
French fries!
AND CHOCOLATE SHAKE!"

THAT ONE climbed on a sofa and shouted:

"Roast potatoes!

Lemon mousse!

Chopped tomatoes!

ORANGE JUICE!"

"Yes!" shouted **THAT ONE**.
"We're having what I WANT!"
they both shouted together.

"You guys better
let me know what
WE want pronto," said Mom,
"or there'll only be time
for a bowl of dry water!"

"I want what I want!"
shouted **THIS ONE**.

"I want what I want, too!"
shouted **THAT ONE**.

"Go and choose the same
or you won't get to play,"
said Mom firmly.

"Well I'm going to go and ask Dad!" said **THIS ONE**.

"Well so am I," said **THAT ONE**,
and they went out in the yard and down the path
to find Big Jim - who was planting out some catnip.

"Dad, Dad, Mom said
we had to decide on the
same thing for lunch.
It's my turn and I want ....

…Cheese pies,
And toffee cake,
French fries,
And chocolate shake ….
…. but **THAT ONE** won't let
me!" said **THIS ONE**.

"But it's my turn and I want …
Roast potatoes,
Lemon mousse,
Chopped tomatoes,
Orange juice,"
said **THAT ONE**.

Big Jim scratched his ears and said:
"Seems like you two guys need to discuss this
so you can agree. Why don't you go and sit by
that old bumble bee tree and sort things out."

THIS ONE and **THAT ONE** went and sat by the tree.

"Cheese Pies!" grumbled **THIS ONE**.

"Roast Potatoes!" said **THAT ONE**.

Then they heard a little voice behind them.

"You'll get no food while you're in this mood!" it said.

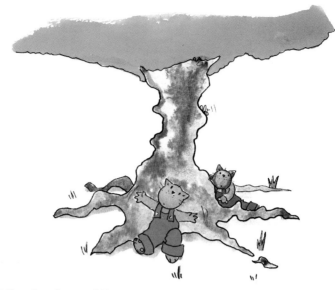

"Who's there?" said **THIS ONE** looking around.

"What was it?" said **THAT ONE** looking up.

"Where are you?" said **THIS ONE**
and **THAT ONE** together.

"Can't agree? There'll be no tea!"
Now it was above them.

THIS ONE and **THAT ONE** looked high and low.

"Make it fair! You've got to share!"
The voice was under
the flower pot!

"If we lift the pot together we
can find who it is," said **THIS ONE**.

The kittens lifted up the pot -
and there was a little bumble bee.

"Work as one and have more fun!" she buzzed.

"Be a winner, get some dinner!"

she buzzed again and flew around them.

"What do you mean?" asked **THIS ONE** and **THAT ONE**.

"When you have a sharing choice, listen to your caring voice!"

and with that the bumble bee flew away into the trees.

THIS ONE and **THAT ONE** sat down on the bench to think. After a long time **THIS ONE** said:

"Maybe if we had what I want today we could have what you want tomorrow?"

"Or we could have what I want today and what you want tomorrow," said **THAT ONE** .

"Or……"

"…. OR WE COULD SHARE!"
they shouted together.

THIS ONE and **THAT ONE** rushed back up the path, past the pots, past Dad, past the catnip and straight to Mom in the kitchen.

"So guys have you made up your mind?"
asked Mom.

"Yes!" shouted **THIS ONE** and **THAT ONE** together.
"We're going to share!

We want .... Fried pies,
And Roast cake,

Orange fries,
And French shake!

Toffee potatoes,

Chopped mousse,

Lemon tomatoes,

And Cheesy juice!"

Lady Jane looked amazed.

"Kits, it's great you decided on sharing and caring
.... but Toffee Potatoes sound just a bit yucky!
And Fried Pies with Roast Cake will taste awful!
Orange flavored French Fries? With Cheesy
juice? I don't think so my sweet kittens!" she laughed.

"I don't want you to get sick so maybe I better decide.
Today it's going to be ….

    Cheese pies,

    Lemon mousse,

    French fries,

    And orange juice!

And tomorrow it'll be ….

    Roast potatoes,

    And toffee cake,

    Chopped tomatoes,

    And chocolate shake!"

    "You're the best, Mom,"
      said **THIS ONE**.

    "And the cleverest,"
      said **THAT ONE**.